FROM BEYOND THE ARCTIC

Tracy Blom

Illustrated by: Sabereh M. Monavar

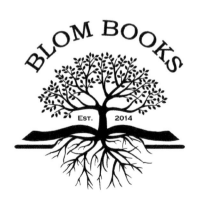

The sky was full of stars; the land was cold and bleak.

The world was full of troubles, of which nobody would speak.

From there in my watchtower, I heard something in the night.

A magic tune came blaring, although no one was in sight.

I ran down to the water, and I saw with my two eyes,

A silver ship and two girls who were surely in disguise.

Their ship was somehow powered by the song they sang,

And as they stopped, the ship turned off, with a mighty clang!

"I am Lusitania," said the one with rainbow hair.

As the other named Citala danced with arms raised in the air.

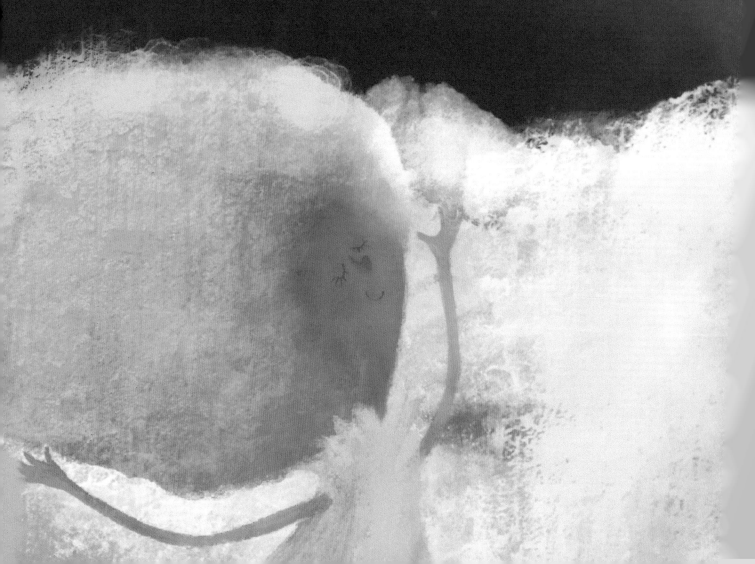

"We hail from Monoceros, on a planet far from here

--- full of happiness and love, unity and cheer.

When a planet calls for help, we seem to hear it first

and only come in times when things are really at their worst."

Citala looked upset and sighed before she said,

"We heard a call from far away and labeled it 'code red.'

The ice here in the Arctic shines a light up to the sky,

But that light is dimming, and we think that we know why."

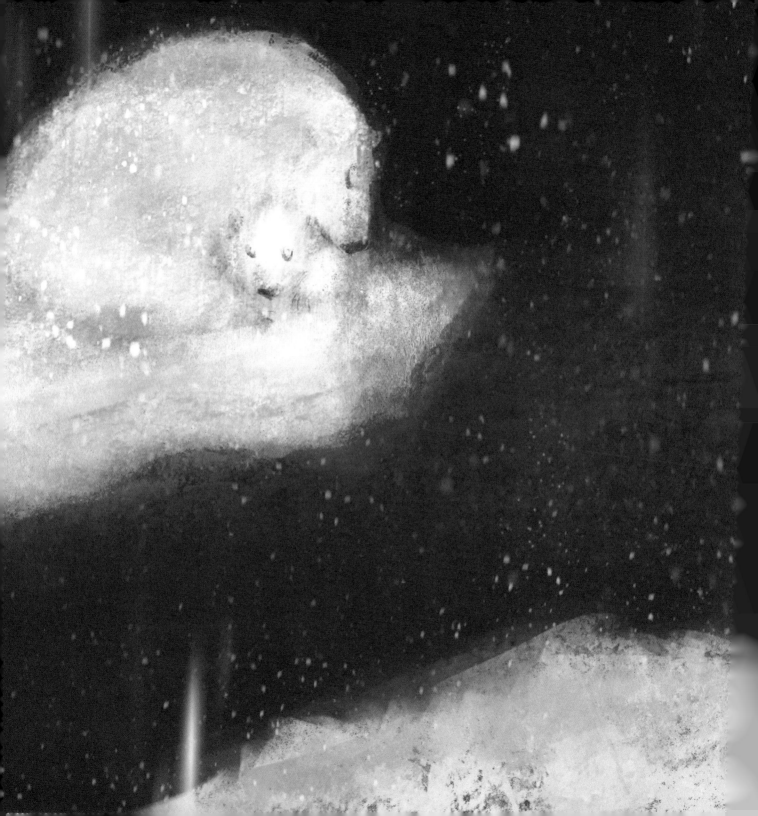

"The ice is melting at a speed that no one can ignore,

And if we don't act fast, it won't be here anymore."

"We found a way to save it and can share our plan with you,"

A bubble appeared within her hands and glowed an icy blue.

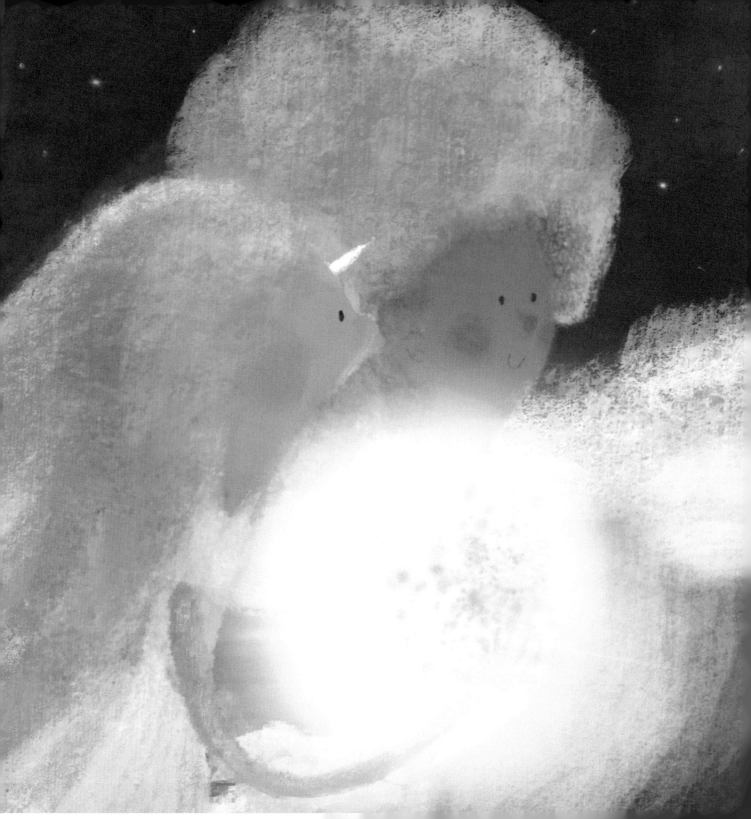

The crystals in this bubble can cover up the snow,

and keep the ice underneath protected down below.

So that when the sun shines down like it does each day,

it will reflect upon the crystals, and the ice won't melt away."

"We can't do this alone, though, and that's where you come in.

This bubble only grows from true happiness within.

So rally up the people! It's time to spread some cheer!"

I laughed, "well, that won't happen, certainly not here."

seems we see more polar bears each and every year,

hich might be great, except they've come to town and now live here.

ey used to be so happy living out there on the ice,

t since their home is vanishing, well... things aren't so nice."

"With the ice caps melting, you can see the lack of seals,

And now the bears have come to town in search of easier meals.

As you can see, our village is in quite a deal of trouble,

I don't think you'll find much joy here to help you grow your bubble."

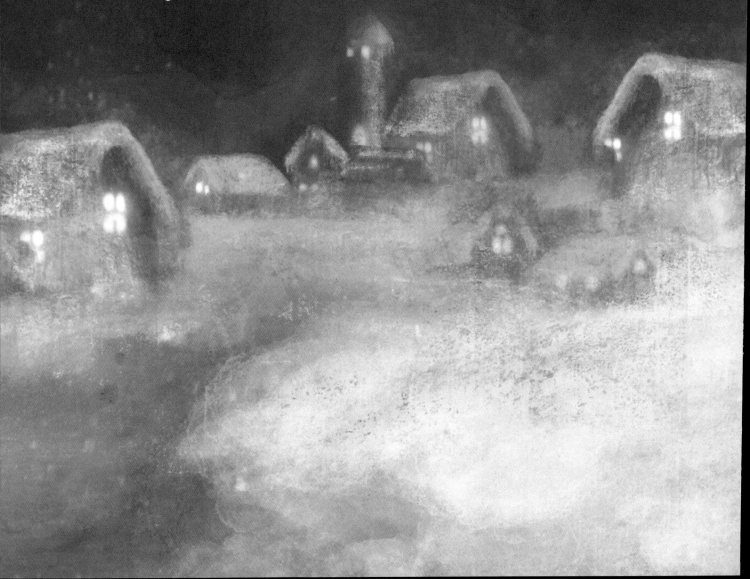

Citala started singing a great enchanting tune,

As the bubble rose to the sky like an air balloon.

The people they came running, mostly out of fright,

and stood along the water's edge gazing at the light.

Some people hid away, some pointed, and some sneered,

And then there was a single child who clapped aloud and cheered.

Soon the crowd was swaying, holding hands, and singing too!

As their joy expanded, the crystal bubble grew!

The people oohed and ahhed and watched with great delight,

As the snowflakes in the bubble twinkled like starlight.

A mighty POP exploded! There were snowflakes all around!

The people danced and cheered as they sealed upon the ground.

"Wait, where are you going?" I cried out with despair,

To the dancing women sailing off into the air.

Citala gave a smile and winked before she said,

"Though we've solved the problem here, Earth is still

code red.'"

Over time the ice restored, and the bears were free to roam,

And they stayed out on the ice since the seals had returned home.

And this time, as I looked out from the tower in my chair,

I smiled at the healthy, happy, mighty polar bear.

Dedication

Dr. Leslie Field, Founder and CTO of Arctic Ice Project

The magical crystals featured in this story were inspired by the work of Dr. Leslie Field, Founder and CTO of the Arctic Ice Project (formerly Ice911 Research). Dr. Field is a Lecturer at Stanford University and the Founder of SmallTech Consulting, LLC. Her work includes Arctic Ice Restoration, teaching at Stanford, and consulting in Microelectromechanical Systems (MEMS) and Nanotech. To learn more Dr. Field and her work, visit: https://www.arcticiceproject.org/

Printed in Great Britain
by Amazon